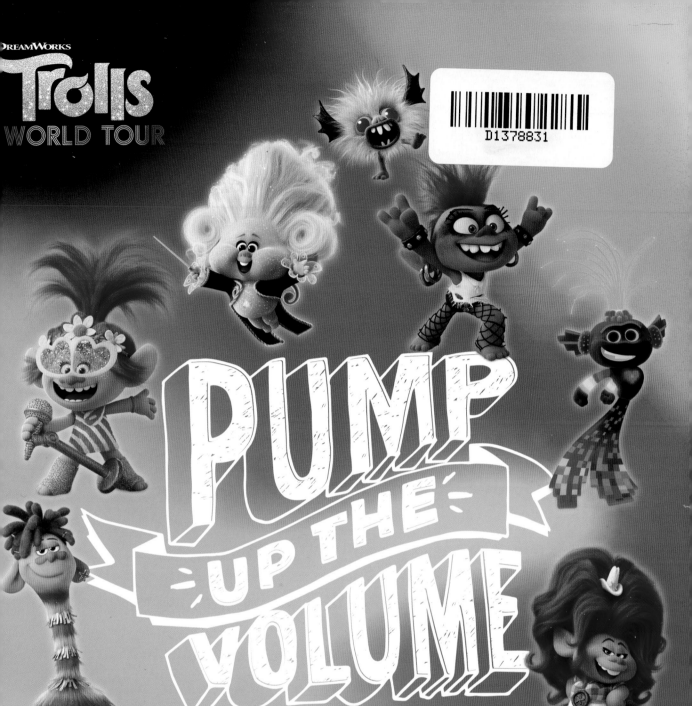

# PUMP UP THE VOLUME

### By Rachel Chlebowski

A GOLDEN BOOK · NEW YORK

ISBN 978-0-593-12783-4

rhcbooks.com

MANUFACTURED IN CHINA

10 9 8 7 6 5 4 3 2 1

# Flower Power

Poppy is the leader of the Trolls in Trolls Village. As their queen, she wears a special flower crown. Draw and use your stickers to make a flower crown of your own!

# Shiny and New!

Poppy has a new friend! Unscramble the letters to find out what his name is.

# NYIT MOADDIN

| | | | | | | | | | | |
|---|---|---|---|---|---|---|---|---|---|---|
| | | | | | | | | | | |

**How many words can you make from the letters in his name? Write as many as you can on a separate sheet of paper!**

See pages 31–32 for all answers.

# The Six Strings

Long ago, the Trolls' ancestors had six strings, each for a different type of music. Can you match each instrument to its Troll and each Troll to its music genre?

**Queen Barb**
**ROCK**

**Trollzart**
**CLASSICAL**

**King Trollex**
**TECHNO**

**Poppy**
**POP**

**Prince D**
**FUNK**

**Delta Dawn**
**COUNTRY**
**WESTERN**

# Musicality Quiz

What type of Troll are you?
Take this quiz to find out.

**1. My dream home is**
A) a golden city.
B) in a colorful forest.
C) inside a volcano!
D) out of this world—
   in a spaceship!
E) an underwater fortress!
F) someplace warm and dry.

**2. My favorite thing to do is**
A) toot my horn and conduct
   an orchestra.
B) dance, hug, and sing!
C) rock out and dominate!
D) find my family.
E) drop the beat!
F) work hard and protect
   the ones I love.

**3. My favorite outfit is**
A) something elegant, with lace!
B) all of them!
C) something edgy and torn-up.
D) anything with sequins
   and glitter!
E) lit up and glowing.
F) patchwork and denim—
   something I can rock in!

**4. I can't go outside
without my**
A) curly hair or long coat.
B) flower crown.
C) adorable pet! Even if she snarls
   at others.
D) favorite pair of golden earrings.
E) inner light and love of electronic
   dance music.
F) favorite hat!

# Make a poster for your kind of music!

# Map Quest

The ancestral Trolls grew to dislike each other's music, so they divided the strings and created the tribes that have lived separately ever since. Can you complete this map of the Troll tribes with your stickers?

# Draw yourself as a Rocker Troll on tour!
## Which instrument do you play?

Page 2

Page 7

Page 3

Page 12

TROLLS
WORLD TOUR

Page 27

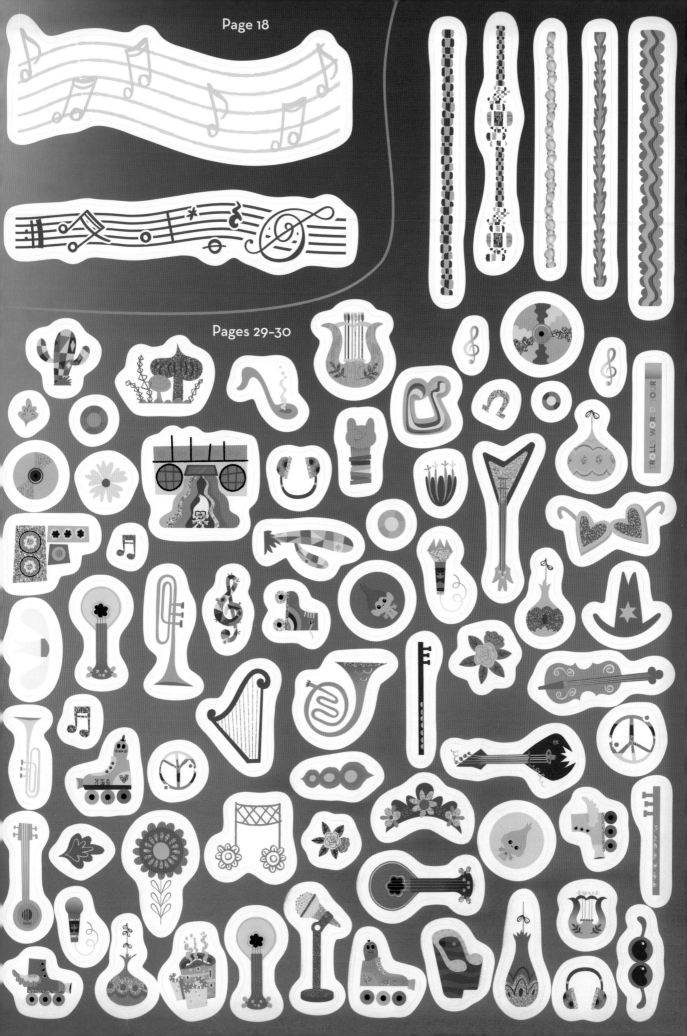

Page 18

Pages 29-30

# Poppy receives an invitation.
## Use the key to decode the name of the messenger bat.

| B | D | E | I |
|---|---|---|---|

# Who sent Poppy the invitation? Follow the letters along the correct path and write them in the boxes.

START

FINISH

# Who's Rocking Who?

Barb wants to control all music. She plans to steal the other
five strings and make everyone Rocker Trolls! She has her pet bat,
Debbie, and right-hand drummer, Riff, by her side.
Which two photos are an exact match?

# Taking Flight!

Poppy is excited to meet all the different Trolls and unite. Use your stickers to add more flair to Sheila B! Poppy and her best friend, Branch, are ready to fly off in the hot-air balloon!

# Do the Wave!

King Trollex is the upbeat leader of the Techno Trolls, a tribe of mermaid Trolls who live underwater. He has many royal duties, but which is the most important? To find out, change each letter below to the one that comes after it in the alphabet. Write the letters in the boxes.

## CQNOOHMF SGD ADZS

# Use the key to color by number!

1 = hot pink • 2 = orange • 3 = yellow • 4 = lime green
5 = light blue • 6 = indigo • 7 = violet

# Techno Tunes

Find all the words in the puzzle!

DJ BOOTH · SPOTLIGHTS · EQUALIZER · TECHNO TROLLS ·
ELECTRONIC · DANCE MUSIC · UNDERWATER · DUBSTEP

```
S R Z H I S E R L C E M
S L E L E C T R O N I C H P
L E M E S D I A P Y O S T Y A H
C D B I L M A E H R E U M K J J
D J P O O M B R L T J M D E W R
I B B A Q D A L U B C E G L P R
T O N A E S S P B D D C A D S I
N O E O U N D E T Z P N L R P T
Z T F A R B N T E J C A S O O R
P H R D E F I S P W L D F N T U
R E N B T S Y B O K E E W C L S
R L G E A G O U I D E K L A I S
C H O K W Q I D C E D Z D D G J
S L L O R T O N H C E T Q U H H
I B M N E U O D X S L E G D T M
S F S A D L L O R T O N H C S T
V U T D N S Y Y L N I B I K G E
M E Q U A L I Z E R W H U K
T F D U A T R M C A T I
```

15

# The Classical Trolls have especially swirly Troll hair. Give Trollzart a great new hairstyle!

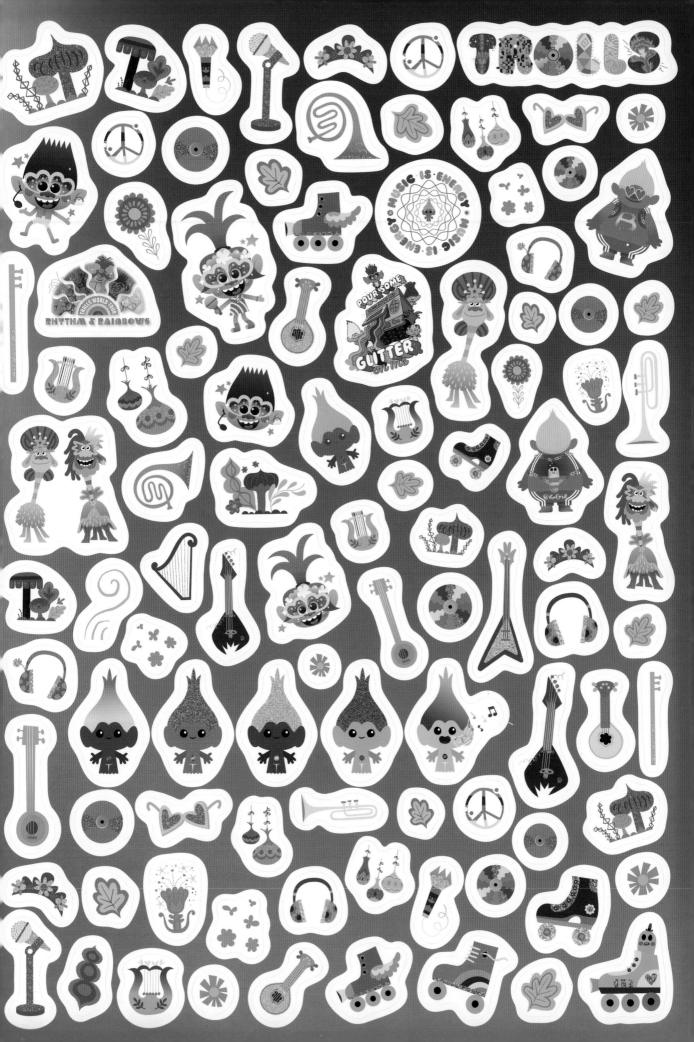

**The Classical Trolls play sophisticated music
with elegant instruments in Symphonyville.
How many instruments can you count on this page?**

**Music is based on repeating patterns.
Follow the patterns and finish each with stickers!**

BONUS: How many musical notes can you place on this page?

# Classical Word Quest

Find a path through the word grid using the words and phrases listed below. Go up, down, forward, and backward (but not diagonally). Use the final letter in each word or phrase to start the next one listed. See how many words you can make from the fifteen leftover letters!

WOLFGANG • GOLDEN STRING • GOSSAMER WINGS • SOPRANO ORCHESTRA • AMADEUS • SYMPHONYVILLE • ELEGANT • TROLLZART

| START | W | O | L | F | I | N | G | O | S | S |
|-------|---|---|---|---|---|---|---|---|---|---|
| | G | N | A | G | R | A | I | W | S | A |
| | O | C | N | S | T | G | N | R | E | M |
| | L | D | E | I | C | S | O | P | L | A |
| | S | M | A | R | T | S | E | R | A | N |
| | D | A | S | I | C | E | H | C | R | O |
| | E | L | M | P | H | E | V | I | L | U |
| | U | S | Y | C | O | N | Y | E | L | M |
| | O | R | T | N | A | G | E | L | A | L |
| | L | L | Z | A | R | T | | | FINISH | |

**HELPFUL HINT:** Try working backward from FINISH!

19

# SQUARE DANCE

## (For 2 players)

With a friend, take turns connecting two dots with a straight line. If the line you draw completes a box, put your initials in it and take another turn. Count one point for boxes containing your initials. If a box you completed contains a Troll, give yourself two points. When all the dots have been connected, the player with more points wins!

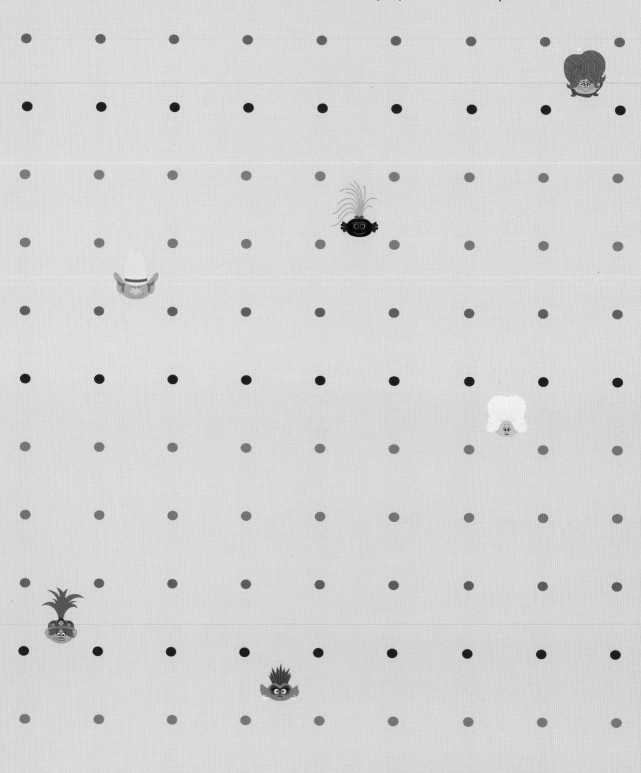

# Rematch!

Play again, double or nothing! If you complete a box with a Troll, give yourself four points. When all the dots have been connected, the player with more points wins!

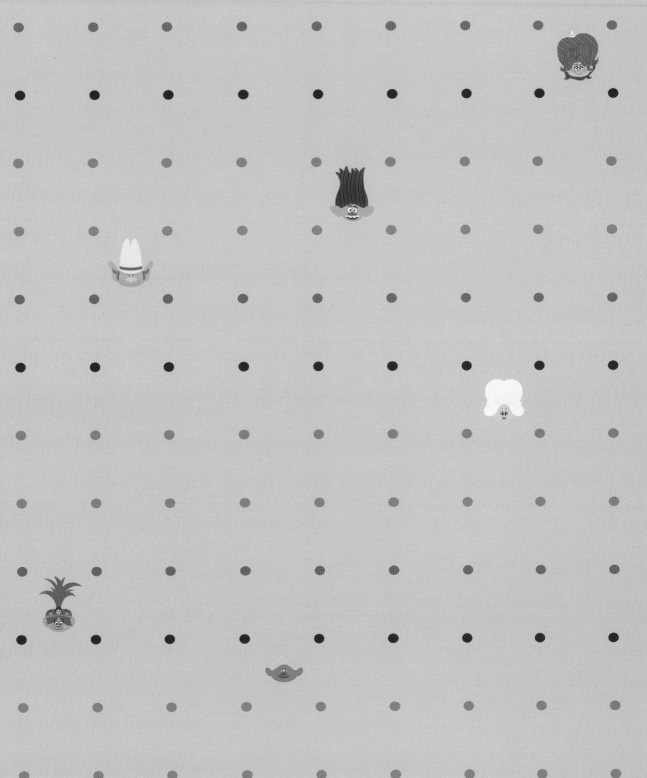

In Lonesome Flats, the heartland of the Country Western Trolls, the houses look like patchwork-quilted cacti. Connect the dots to create a home for Mayor Delta Dawn. Then color it in!

# Hat's It To Ya!

Use stickers to put the right hat on Delta Dawn.
What would you look like as a Country Western Troll?
Draw yourself in the space provided—and don't forget your hat!

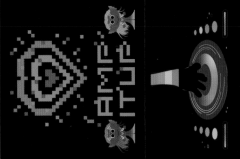

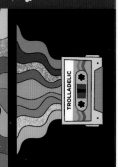

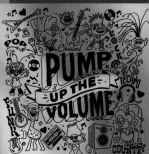

# Funk Family

While searching for Trolls who might look like him, Cooper gets drawn up into a shiny spaceship. Solve the maze to reunite Cooper with his family—Vibe City's King Quincy, Queen Essence, and Prince D!

START

FINISH

# Design your own album cover with your stickers!

# Scrapbooking for Everyone!

Cut out these items for the starter scrapbook on the next page. Use a photo in the frame to make yourself part of the music!

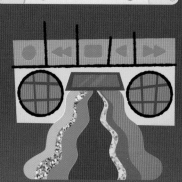

TROLLS WORLD TOUR

:: VIP LOUNGE ::

GREAT VIBES

TROLLS WORLD TOUR

POP

*Trollzart*

TROLLS WORLD TOUR

CLASSICAL

ROCK

QUEEN BARB

TROLLS WORLD TOUR

**TROLLS WORLD TOUR**

Cooper

# Funk

**COUNTRY**

★

TROLLS
WORLD
TOUR

*Delta Dawn*

**TROLLS WORLD TOUR**

# TECHNO

TROLLEX

# ANSWERS

## Page 3

Tiny Diamond

**Possible answers:** and, any, dad, day, dot, main, many, mind, mint, moat, not, tan, tin, toy

## Page 4

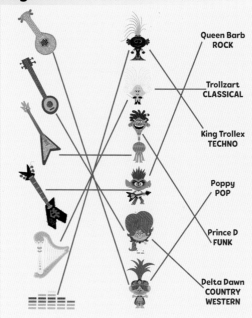

Queen Barb **ROCK**

Trollzart **CLASSICAL**

King Trollex **TECHNO**

Poppy **POP**

Prince D **FUNK**

Delta Dawn **COUNTRY WESTERN**

## Page 5

If you answered mostly A, you're a Classical Troll like Trollzart!

If you answered mostly B, you're a Pop Troll like Poppy!

If you answered mostly C, you're a Rocker Troll like Barb!

If you answered mostly D, you're a Funk Troll like Cooper (or Prince D)!

If you answered mostly E, you're a Techno Troll like Trollex!

If you answered mostly F, you're a Country Western Troll like Delta Dawn!

## Page 7

## Page 9

Debbie

## Page 10

Queen Barb of the Rocker Trolls

## Page 11
A and D

## Page 13
Dropping the beat

## Page 15

## Page 17
21

## Page 19

Possible answers: all, call, calm, clam, class, classical, lime, mail, meal, mice, mile, music, musical, seal

## Page 26